THE BEST FRIEND

Story by G. Walton Williams
Illustrations by John Kollock

NORMAN S. BERG, PUBLISHER
"SELLANRAA"
DUNWOODY, GEORGIA

For
George Walton
and
Ellison Adger
and
William Aiken
and
Edward Dean

A long time ago—
about one hundred and fifty years ago—

in the city of Charleston
in South Carolina,

a group of merchants came together to talk about their troubles.
Business was bad, and they did not
know what to do about it. All that
they knew was that they needed a
good friend to help them out of
their troubles.

Cotton planters in South Carolina and Georgia were shipping their cotton to Savannah and not to Charleston. This made the Charleston merchants sad.

They decided they would lay a railroad track to Augusta—though it was a great distance away—140 miles—and they would bring their cotton to Charleston by trains drawn by steam locomotives — though no locomotive had ever traveled so great a distance.

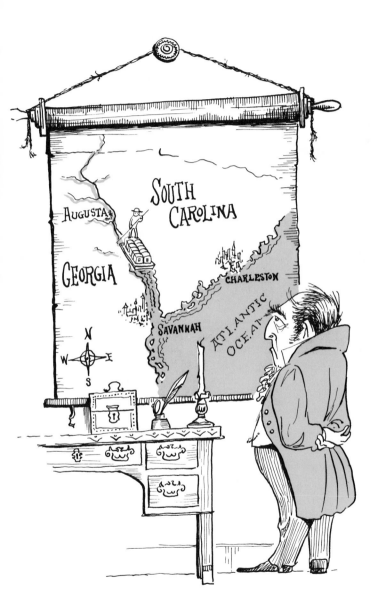

One young inventor tried to persuade the merchants to use the wind and sails instead of a steam locomotive to draw their trains. He built a wagon with a sail to prove he was right.

But the wind was too high. It blew away the sail and proved he was wrong.

Another inventor suggested they should use a horse running on a treadmill to make the power to draw their trains.

But a third inventor told the merchants that there was no reason to expect any improvement in the breed of horses

but that the person was not living
who knew what the breed of locomotives would place at the com-
mand of man.

With this thought in their minds, the merchants ordered a steam locomotive for their railroad. It was built in New York and sent by boat to Charleston. It was the first locomotive built in America for service on a railroad.

The merchants hoped that this locomotive would be the friend they needed. They called it THE BEST FRIEND.

The locomotive had been taken apart before it was shipped from New York; it was put back together in Charleston,

and was soon ready to run on the track which had now been laid a part of the way to Augusta.

The engine of the Best Friend was
a vertical boiler with a fire box
underneath it. The fuel for the fire
was wood. The boiler was equipped
with a safety valve that let out the
extra steam when the fire became
too hot. The Best Friend carried a
crew of two—an engineer and a fireman.

At nine o'clock in the morning of Christmas Day 1830, the Best Friend made its first official run on the track. It was an exciting time. A military band played for the occasion, and a detachment of soldiers fired a gun salute to the new iron horse as it began to run its race.

One of the passengers described the trip like this: "We flew away on the wings of the wind at the speed of 20 miles per hour, leaving all the world behind. The locomotive darted forth like a rocket, scattering sparks and flame on either side, passed over a creek, hop, step, and jump, and landed us all safe at the station before we had time to be scared."

For several months the Best Friend
pulled trains of freight and passengers through the countryside. The
locomotive was a great success and
brought both business and pleasure
to the merchants who had invited
their new friend to come and live
with them.

One day when it was six months old, the Best Friend was resting at the station after a long hard pull.

It was a hot June day; there was a hot fire in the fire box; there was hot steam in the boiler. Every few minutes the safety valve went WHOOSH and let out the extra steam.

The fireman was having his lunch after working hard in the hot sun all morning.

The WHOOSH of the steam as it came through the safety valve kept the fireman from enjoying his lunch in peace and quiet.

He tied down the safety valve with his pocket handkerchief.

Now the steam could not escape
from the boiler any longer. Instead,
the boiler grew hotter and hotter,
redder and redder, until

it burst.

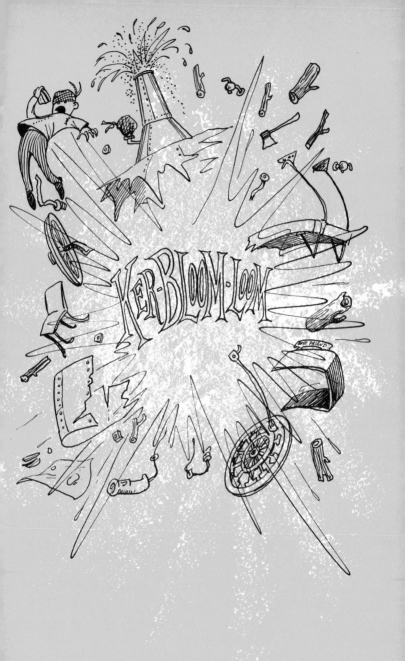

When the smoke and steam cleared away there was not much of the Best Friend left to be seen.

The merchants picked up all the pieces and brought them back to the workshop.

They decided to rebuild their good friend and put her back on the tracks as soon as possible. But they gave her a new shape and a new name. She was called

THE PHOENIX.

People did not want to ride behind
a locomotive that might explode
again and blow them all into pieces,

and so the merchants told them
how safe they would be in the fu-
ture because

right behind the Phoenix would be
a freight car loaded with bales of
cotton to protect them.

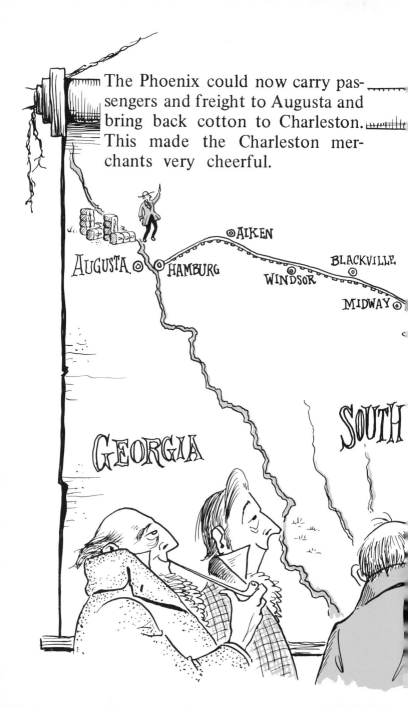

The Phoenix could now carry passengers and freight to Augusta and bring back cotton to Charleston. This made the Charleston merchants very cheerful.

AIKEN

AUGUSTA   HAMBURG   BLACKVILLE

WINDSOR

MIDWAY

GEORGIA

SOUTH

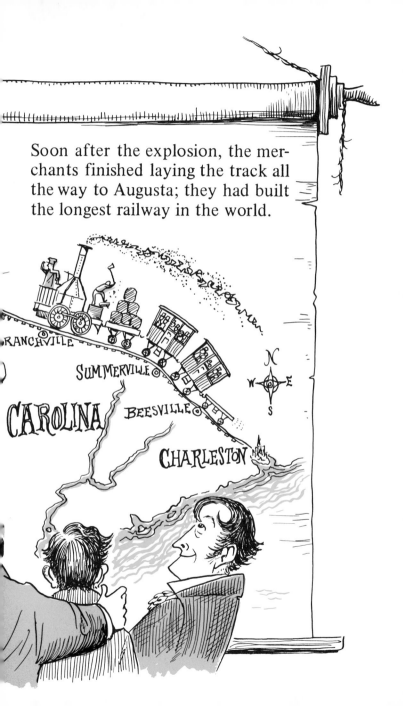

Soon after the explosion, the merchants finished laying the track all the way to Augusta; they had built the longest railway in the world.

In Charleston, business began to improve. But the Best Friend and the Phoenix had done more than merely help the Charleston merchants, they had shown to all the world that a steam locomotive could pull a train over a long railway. They had begun the railroad age.

The South Carolina Canal and Railroad Company was chartered in 1827 as a means of securing for Charleston the commerce of the upcountry of South Carolina and Georgia, chiefly the exporting of cotton. As it was much easier to float cotton down the river to Savannah by flat boat than to bring it to Charleston by wagon train, Savannah flourished and Charleston declined. The Company sought to divert the trade of the upland planters and bring their crop directly to Charleston by railroad.

Construction on the road began in January 1830, and the first locomotive was ordered from the West Point Foundry in New York City in the same year. This locomotive, called The Best Friend, was the first locomotive built in America for service on a railroad.

The Best Friend made several trial runs in December 1830, and on Christmas Day regular passenger service was begun. The description quoted in the text recounts the thrills and wonders of that day as the train raced at 21 miles per hour along the six miles of track that had been laid. In June 1831, the locomotive boiler exploded, and the Best Friend was no more. It was rebuilt as the Phoenix and ran on the road for many years thereafter.

In October 1833, the last section of track was laid to Hamburg (across the river from Augusta), completing a railroad of 136 miles in length, the longest railroad in the world at that time. Trains on this road were the first in America to carry the mails. The Company later became one of the constituent companies of The Southern Railway System.